TONY BALONEY

Buddy Trouble

P9-CRG-790

BY
PAM MUÑOZ RYAN

ILLUSTRATED BY
EDWIN FOTHERINGHAM

SCHOLASTIC INC.

To Ruby, Levi, and Sadie —P.M.R.

To my family: Becky, Anna, and Joe —E.F.

Library of Congress Cataloging-in-Publication Data Available

ISBN 978-0-545-48170-0
12 11 10 9 8 7 6 5 4 3 2 1   13 14 15 16 17
Printed in the U.S.A.   40
First paperback printing, February 2014

The text in this book was set in Adobe Caslon Pro Regular.
The display type was set in P22 Kane. The title was hand lettered by Edwin Fotheringham.
The illustrations were created using digital media.
Book design by Marijka Kostiw

CONTENTS

Daphne and Velma help Scooby and Shaggy warm up.

SHERIFF! WHAT ARE YOU DOING HERE?

I AM LOOKING FOR THE SNOW MONSTER.

18

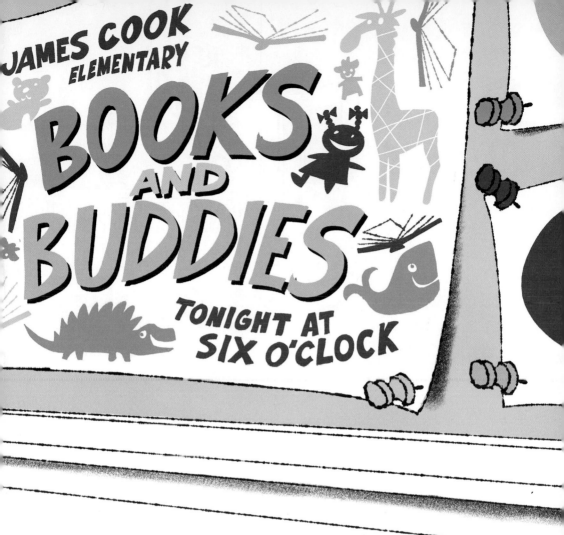

BEST BEHAVIOR

Tony Baloney, the macaroni penguin,

and his best friend, Bob, are excited.

Tonight is Books and Buddies.

The whole school is invited!

Their teacher, Mrs. Gamboney,
reminds them to bring a cozy blanket
and a favorite stuffed animal or doll.
She says, "We'll turn the Everything Room
into a campground, and the teachers
will read stories by flashlight!"
Tony Baloney and Bob plan to bring
their best stuffed animal buddies,
Dandelion and Pedro.

6

"Dandelion is a little afraid of the dark,"

 says Tony Baloney.

"Pedro is too," says Bob.

"Let's promise to camp next to each other,"

 says Tony Baloney.

7

After school, Tony Baloney

has a little talk with Dandelion.

Momma and Poppa said we have to be on Best Behavior all afternoon if we want to go to Books and Buddies. That's the rule.

I will ooze politeness.

No fighting with Big Sister.

I'm a lover, not a fighter.

Tonight will be so much fun! Mrs. Gamboney said she's reading *Elephant Seal on a Ferris Wheel*.

That's our favorite book!

Group hug!

At snack, Momma Baloney says,

"I am taking the babies to their playgroup.

I want you two to pick up your toys before

we go to Books and Buddies."

"I'll start now!" offers Tony Baloney.

Big Sister Baloney is bossier than usual.

"Sort the crayons by *color*," she says.

"Good idea," says Tony Baloney.

"Trucks go in one bin, puppets in another."

"Thanks for reminding me," says Tony Baloney.

"I'll put away the doll clothes,"

declares Big Sister Baloney.

"Be my guest," says Tony Baloney.

"The glitter goes in the craft box,"

hisses Big Sister Baloney.

Tony Baloney's politeness fades.

"I can put it on the shelf if I want," he says.

"That's not where it *goes*," says Big Sister Baloney.

"That's not where it *goes*," he mimics.

"Stop copying me!"

"Stop copying me!"

"You're so annoying."

"You're so annoying."

"*I'll* put it away!" orders Big Sister Baloney.

Tony Baloney does *not* love trouble . . .

. . . but trouble *loves* him.

DISASTER

"This is *not* Best Behavior,"

says Momma Baloncy.

Poppa Baloney shakes his head.

"And you know the rule."

Tony wails, "But I *promised* Bob!"

Big Sister Baloney cries,

"And I'm a flashlight helper!"

Momma and Poppa Baloney stand firm.

When Tony Baloney isn't looking,

Big Sister Baloney seeks revenge.

Big Sister Baloney mutters to herself,

"We have to miss the best school event ever,

and it's *all your fault*."

"*You're* the one who started it,"

says Tony Baloney.

"Don't talk to me!"

says Big Sister Baloney.

"Don't worry, I'm never

talking to you again.

I'll go talk to Dandelion."

Big Sister Baloney smirks

and says, "Be my guest."

LOST AND FOUND

Tony Baloney looks for his best buddy,

but he cannot find him anywhere.

"Poppa!" yells Tony Baloney.

Poppa Baloney and Tony Baloney

search for Dandelion.

They look in the kitchen.

They look in the bedrooms.

They look in Tony Baloney's hide-y space.

They look . . .

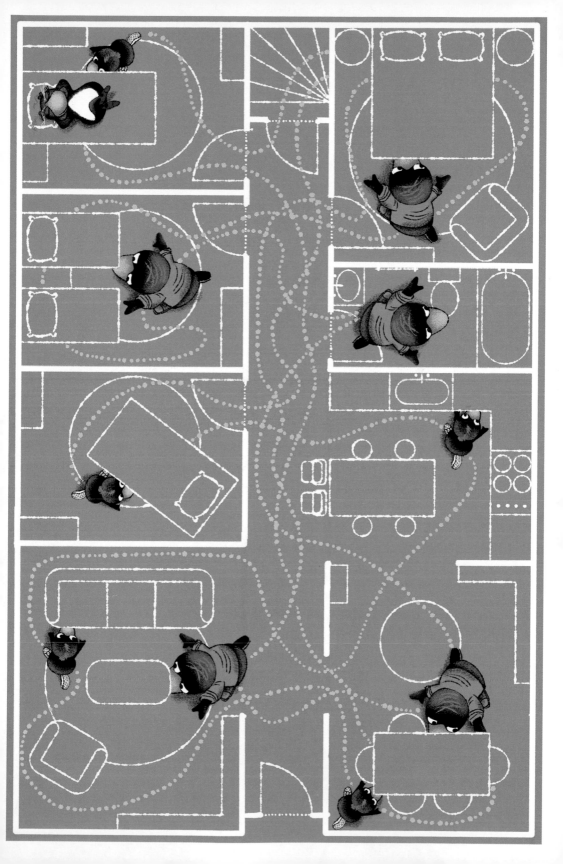

. . . at Big Sister Baloney.

She says sweetly, "Maybe

Dandelion was misplaced."

Poppa Baloney gives her *the look*.

Big Sister Baloney confesses,

"Well . . . I accidentally, or maybe on purpose,

put him in the diaper bag."

Tony Baloney's eyes shoot arrows.

"Dandelion is *scared*

of the diaper bag!"

Poppa Baloney, Big Sister Baloney,

and Tony Baloney have a heart-to-heart talk.

Tony Baloney takes a break
in his room. "And Poppa said
that we're going to be brother and sister
for *the rest of our lives*,
which is a really long time.
And that it would be more fun
if we tried to be friends sometimes,
instead of always arguing.
But . . . *sniff* . . . she put Dandelion
in the *diaper bag*, and I don't think
I can forgive her. Ever."

After a week, or maybe only an hour,
Momma Baloney arrives home with
the Bothersome Babies Baloney.

Tony Baloney unzips the diaper bag
and looks inside.
It is not a pretty sight.

Tony Baloney picks up his buddy.

What happened to you?

My worst fears came true.
It was Princess Day
at playgroup.

You're so . . . pink.

And I'm *allergic* to pink!
Do you see a rash?
Am I swollen?

No rash. But what's that *smell*?

Oh, spit-up or tushy ointment or poopy diapers. It's a stinkin' mystery.

WARM AND FUZZY

Tony Baloney sprays Dandelion

with spot remover and puts him

into the washing machine.

He adds the detergent.

Glug, glug, glug.

He adds a little more detergent,

or maybe too much.

Big Sister Baloney comes to the rescue.

She mops up the suds.

She rinses Dandelion up and down

and wrings out the water.

She stays with Tony Baloney

and watches Dandelion go

around and around and around

in the dryer.

"It's like a little merry-go-round.

This is probably more fun for Dandelion

than Books and Buddies,"

says Big Sister Baloney.

After four hours, or

maybe only forty minutes,

Dandelion is clean and fluffy.

Tony Baloney is so grateful

that he and Dandelion

give Big Sister Baloney . . .

. . . a group hug.

"I know, I know," she says.

"I'm fabulous. But *please*,

enough already with the

little brother germs."

Momma and Poppa have a change of heart.

"We like how you cooperated,"

   says Momma Baloney.

"And because you cleaned up and made up

   all on your own, we've decided that you

   may go to Books and Buddies,"

   says Poppa Baloney.

Tony Baloney and Big Sister Baloney cheer.

At school, everything looks
magical in the dark.